This book belongs to

_____

Published by Advance Publishers
© 1998 Disney Enterprises, Inc.
All rights reserved. Printed in the United States.
No part of this book may be reproduced or copied in any form
without the written permission of the copyright owner.

Written by Ronald Kidd
Illustrated by Kevin Kidney and Jody Daily
Produced by Bumpy Slide Books

ISBN: 1-57973-014-0

10 9 8 7 6 5 4 3 2

One day in Never Land, Peter Pan and his friends were playing Follow the Leader. The followers were John, Michael, Wendy, Tinker Bell, and the Lost Boys. The leader, as usual, was Peter.

He led them over rocks, around trees, and through a hollow log until they came to a rippling, gurgling stream.

"Come on, everybody," Peter called. "We're going to cross the stream — but let's do it the fun way!"

Grabbing a rope, he swung out over the water and landed on the other side. One by one his friends followed, until only John was left.

"Tallyho!" John cried, and he leapt for the rope. He missed and fell into the stream.

As Michael helped him out of the water, John grumbled, "Why does Peter always have to be in charge? Just once I'd like to do things my way!"

They rejoined the group, but John had started thinking. He wanted to show Peter how brave and clever he was, and for that he needed a plan. Finally, farther down the trail, John stopped.

"By Jove," he cried, "I've got it!"

"Got what?" asked Michael.

John said, "You'll see." He took Michael's hand, and together they slipped off into the forest.

Not far away, a pirate ship was anchored in the harbor. High above the deck, the lookout had fallen asleep, which was why he didn't see a rowboat making its way toward the ship. In the boat were John and Michael, dressed as pirates.

"Are we there yet?" asked Michael.

"Just a little bit farther," said John. "Then we'll spy on Captain Hook and take the information back to Peter. Won't that be exciting?"

Michael yawned. "I guess so. Can I take a nap now?"

"No!" said John. "Spies don't take naps."

As the boys reached the pirate ship, they heard a ticking sound.

"What's that?" asked Michael. Just then, a pair of beady eyes poked up out of the water.

"Be careful!" John exclaimed. "It's the Crocodile!"

But John needn't have worried. Years ago the Crocodile had swallowed Captain Hook's hand, and ever since, the only person he wanted to catch was Hook. The Crocodile probably would have succeeded by now, but he had also swallowed an alarm clock, and its ticking served as a warning to the captain.

John and Michael climbed up over the side of
the ship to the sound of footsteps approaching.
Looking around desperately, John spotted two mops
and a bucket. He whispered to Michael, "Just do as
I do. And whatever happens, don't cry!"

Around the corner came Smee, the first mate. "My goodness, look what we have here," said Smee. "Pirates, working!"

Sure enough, John and Michael were busy scrubbing the deck, trying not to show their faces.

"Can't say that I remember you," Smee went on. "But whoever you are, you're doing a fine job!" Then he hurried off to check on some supplies.

When Smee was gone, John turned to Michael. "Well done!" he said. "Now we've got some spying to do."

Finding a telescope, John climbed up the rigging. "What are you looking for?" asked Michael.

John said, "Captain Hook. Surely he's around here someplace."

Just then Smee came walking by. "Well, hello again," said the first mate. "Do you see anything?"

"Uh, well, uh . . . weather!" said John. "A storm, actually, and it's coming this way."

Smee replied, "A storm? I should tell the captain." He hurried off, calling, "Keep up the good work!"

John turned to Michael. "This is perfect. He'll lead us right to Captain Hook!"

They followed Smee at a safe distance and saw him enter a cabin at the front of the ship. John whispered to his brother, "Stand watch. I'll be right back."

When John peered through the porthole of the cabin, he saw Captain Hook. Unfortunately, Captain Hook also saw him. But unlike Smee, Captain Hook was not fooled. He could easily see that John was not a pirate.

"Spies!" thundered Hook. "Get them, Smee!"

"Now we're doomed!" Michael moaned.

"Not necessarily," said John.

The first mate came scuttling out of the cabin. When he saw John and Michael, he said, "Oh, it's you!"

"Indeed it is," said John. "We've been checking the safety of the captain's quarters, and I must say that we're shocked. Why, spies could look through that porthole as easily as I did!"

"Well . . . yes, I suppose you're right," Smee admitted. "Maybe we should talk to the captain about it."

"Do we have to?" asked Michael.

Smee led the boys inside. "What's the meaning of this, Smee?" Captain Hook demanded.

The first mate stammered, "Th-they say they were checking on your safety, sir. And I must say, they're hard workers. Just today I saw them swabbing the deck and standing lookout."

The captain looked John straight in the eye.

"Yes," he agreed, "I think they're doing a fine job. After all, with the attack only three days off, security is more important than ever."

"Attack?" said John.

Hook said, "We've discovered Peter Pan's hideout and will attack in three days." He turned to his first mate. "Release them, Smee. We've got work to do."

As soon as the boys were outside, John whispered
to Michael, "We have to warn Peter! Come with me!"
They climbed over the side of the ship, and a few
moments later they were rowing for shore.

Back on board, Captain Hook laughed as he watched the boys through his telescope. "Yes," he said, "I can trust you — to lead us straight to Pan!"

Smee straightened his glasses. "Y-you mean, sir, they really *were* spies?"

"Of course," said Hook. "They're some of Pan's little friends. They don't know it, but now they're working for us!"

A short time later, John and Michael rowed their boat out of the harbor toward Peter Pan's hideout. "My plan worked!" John said. "We spied on Hook, just as I had hoped. And best of all, we didn't need Peter or anyone else. We did it all by ourselves."

They had just reached the shore when Michael heard something. "Uh-oh," he said. "I hear ticking. Like a clock. Like a clock in a crocodile. Like a clock in the crocodile that follows Captain Hook!"

The boys looked at each other. "Captain Hook?" they said. "Run!"

They scrambled up a hill, with John leading
the way. When he reached the top, he called,
"This way, Michael!"

There was no answer.

"Michael?" said John, looking back.

Halfway down the hill stood Captain Hook. Beside him, Michael struggled in the arms of two pirates.

"Keep going, John!" cried Michael. "Don't stop!"

A few minutes later, John burst into the hideout. Peter, Wendy, and the others gathered around him. "Not only does Captain Hook have Michael," John explained, "he also knows where our hideout is."

Peter shook his head. "If Hook really knew, why did he need to follow you? I think it was a trick."

"He knew we weren't pirates?" asked John.

Peter said, "I'm afraid so."

John groaned. "Peter, I've made a terrible mess of things. What are we going to do?"

"I'm not sure," said Peter. "But whatever we do, let's do it together."

Later, on the pirate ship, Smee tied Michael to a chair.

"It's very simple," Hook told the boy. "Either tell me the location of Pan's hideout, or walk the plank."

"I won't tell," said Michael. "Never!"

As they spoke, a girl's voice came floating
through the porthole. "Captain? Oh, Captain Hook!"
Opening the door of his cabin, Hook saw Wendy
standing on the ship's plank. "Lovely day, isn't it?"
she said pleasantly.

Hook turned to his first mate. "Something's going
on here, Smee. Watch the boy. I'll be right back!"

As soon as Hook was gone, John looked into the porthole.

"Not you again!" Smee exclaimed. He ran out and locked the door behind him. But as he was dropping the key into his pocket, Tinker Bell grabbed it and flew away.

Tinker Bell unlocked the cabin door, and one of the Lost Boys hurried inside. He lifted Michael, chair and all, and passed him to the other Lost Boys, who were standing in a row — out the door, across the deck, over the side of the ship, and into a boat waiting below.

When all the boys were safely in the boat, John got ready to board. With Smee still behind him, he opened his umbrella, leapt over the side of the ship,

and floated down to join them. With John safe,
the Lost Boys cast off and headed for shore.

Meanwhile, on the ship's plank, Captain Hook
reached out to grab Wendy. But suddenly a green
blur streaked through the air and scooped her up.
It was Peter Pan!

"Blast you!" Hook cried.

Next Tinker Bell swooped in front of Hook and
startled him. Hook lost his balance, but at the last
minute he snagged the plank with his hook. As he
dangled there, he noticed a ticking noise.

"Smee!" he shrieked. "Get me out of here!"

Later that evening, Peter and his friends sat
in their hideout, talking about the rescue. "I say,"
said John, "it was smashing, wasn't it?"

Wendy smiled. "That's because all of us helped.
I hope you've learned that things go better when
you're part of a team."

"I certainly have," said John. "But you know,
there's one thing I still don't understand. When

Michael and I met Captain Hook, how did he
know we weren't pirates?"

"It's a small thing," said Peter, "but you may
want to keep it in mind if you ever try this again."

"What's that?" asked John.

Peter grinned and said, "Pirates don't carry
umbrellas."

John went off to be a spy
On Hook's pirate ship.
But then Michael fell into
The captain's evil grip.
Luckily John's trusted friends
Came up with a solution —
When friends work together,
Each one makes a contribution!